The Good Life in a Hilltop Village

Hans Wrang

Published by Hans Wrang, 2024.

THE GOOD LIFE IN A HILLTOP VILLAGE

First edition. April 22, 2024.

Copyright © 2024 Hans Wrang.

ISBN: 979-8224162079

Written by Hans Wrang.

Also by Hans Wrang
The Adventures of Gammelnok
Jesper Knasfis

To all the friends my wife and I have accumulated during the
last twenty years in this village.

This is an attempt to acknowledge the kindness and welcome
we were shown from the very first day in what we now consider
to be 'our village'

Most of the people in this story are real but names have been
changed to protect both the guilty and the innocent.

The setting has been moved back a good sixty years to try to
paint a picture of village life during the Franco regime.

Quite a few of our friends and acquaintances have passed away
since we met them. This is an attempt to honour their memory.
To the ones still among us, I hope you might enjoy reading this
and not take offence if you recognize yourself or if I have
misrepresented your character.

The good life in a hilltop village

A short depiction of life in a remote village during the Franco Regime
by
Hans Wrang

Dedication

To all the friends my wife and I have accumulated during the last twenty years in this village.
This is an attempt to acknowledge the kindness and welcome we were shown from the very first day in what we now consider to be 'our village'
Most of the people in this story are real but names have been changed to protect both the guilty and the innocent.
The setting has been moved back a good sixty years to try to paint a picture of village life during the Franco regime.
Quite a few of our friends and acquaintances have passed away since we met them. This is an attempt to honour their memory. To the ones still among us, I hope you might enjoy reading this and not take offence if you recognize yourself or if I have misrepresented your character.

Chapter 1: The day the music died

We are in a small mountain village in Southern Spain. The year is 1959 and the Month is February. The date: February 3rd. Preparations for the annual Carnival or Carnaval is in full swing. As is tradition in these parts, people group together creating costumes in the same unique design and compose satirical songs to be performed all over the village to large enthusiastic crowds. This year as in previous years while Spain is under the law of El Caudillo everyone has to be careful with their Carnaval activities as the regime is definitively not in favour of satirical performances.

It is believed that this custom goes back centuries, costumes were essential in breaking down social barriers, helping classes to come together, providing freedom from repression. People could let loose, follow their instincts, and dress up as dukes or chimney sweeps, or fantastical creatures. They also had a unique opportunity to make fun of authority without facing charges, against the church, the government, or the ruling classes. This tradition of criticizing and poking fun at famous personalities, such as politicians, singers and actors, remains central to the Carnaval, and even continues throughout the current Franco era when Carnaval is banned, but cities like Cádiz refuses to comply and rebels at the restriction, launching ever more elaborate Carnaval processions. This village follows bravely where Cádiz leads.

The group of friends we are following for this Carnaval have gathered in the house of Luis Payaya which is just off the main upper square, but down one of the many steep side streets which characterize this particular mountain top village. Well, to be correct it was the house of Luis's parents. The youngsters are still in their last year at school but have formed a lasting friendship over the past few years.

They are all keenly aware that in the rest of Europe and in America the world is moving on with singing artists making waves with Rock and Roll and protest songs. All of which is forbidden in Spain. Franco though cannot stop them listening to pirate radio stations like Radio Luxemburg or Danish Radio Mercur which had started transmitting the year before. Building your own Crystal radio set is not difficult and many are secretly in use throughout the village. Smuggled or contraband records are available from relatives or friends living elsewhere in Europe or America.

Rehearsal is well on the way and the group of friends, six in all, gives it their all singing their home composed Carnaval song. Their festive costumes are nearly ready and the big day is looming. Their hopes are high for winning first prize.

Southern Spain and especially Andalusia has a wealth of musical talents ranging from singing and dancing flamenco to playing musical instruments, either in marching bands or in would be rock or pop groups. Rock Andaluz will take another decade to emerge.

Luis is considered the practical joker in the group; Alejandro is the rebel with long hair in a ponytail and a lover of all kind of food. Angel is practical and can turn his hand to creating all kind of things, be it in wood, metal or cloth. Gabriel, known as Gabi among his friends is a keen and accomplished singer of traditional Flamenco music. He is often accompanied by Filipe who plays a mean acoustic guitar. The last member of the group is Daniel, a self-confessed homosexual to his friends, but still hiding in the closet. Daniel is a very generous person, with many friends in the gay community. His sexual orientation is kept strictly secret by the group of friends as it is still a grave sin and an illegal activity frowned on, both by the Franco regime and the Catholic Church.

Rehearsals completed, Luis turns to his Crystal radio set and tunes in to his favourite Radio Luxemburg.

The group watches as his face changes. Tears wells in his eyes. He hands the headphone to Alejandro who immediately looks equally distressed. The group takes it in turn to listen.

This will be known as "The Day the Music Died". Buddy Holly, Ricky Valence and The Big Bopper had all died in an air crash earlier in the day.

These three were the musical heroes of the assembled group of friends and the news hid hard.

Their music had given them all hope in the oppressive and restrictive day to day life in an Andalusian village seemingly cut off from the rest of the world by Fascism and Catholicism.

Leaving Luis's house in a downcast mood, they head for the main square to down a caña in memory of Buddy and Co. The square looks no different from the day before. The fountain in the middle with its four stone lions is still spouting water and a flag is still flying full mast from the balcony of the Ayuntamiento building. The clock in the small tower above is still showing the wrong time.

The group of friends is too miserable for idle chat and agreeing to meet again the following day for rehearsal, they split up.

Luis stays behind to pay the bill.

Chapter 2: A closer look at Luis

After paying the bill, Luis saunters into a close-by charity shop. Wearing his customary cloth cap, he picks up a few items, bags them and carries on down one of the side streets leading to yet another square. This one is more or less rectangular with a raised section in the centre where a much welcome shade is provided by the four huge laurel trees growing there, one in each corner. They are so old that their roots are beginning to lift the paving stones around their trunks. Surrounded by dwellings and a single bar on three sides, the massive Parish Church completes and dominates the north side.

The church does not interest Luis much, not being overly religious. He has of course had to attend numerous events inside this magnificent building; His own baptism which he does not remember, his first communion which he does remember, having to dress up in a borrowed sailor's suit. And last year's Easter procession where he was chosen to be one of the seventy-two Portadores or Costaleros to carry the Throne of Nuestro Padre Jesús Nazareno de Las Torres. The Throne had been enormously heavy and the many hours it took to complete the route had worn him out. The going had been slow, stopping at the sound of the controller's bell to signal a rest. Five rings of the bell to get ready again, one ring to lift and finally one ring to start moving. The Village dignitaries had led the procession carrying ceremonial staffs. The ladies allowed to participate, were wearing tall black lace mantillas secured by large combs. One or two of his fellow Portadores had worn black blindfolds to amplify the experience of suffering.

Luis sits on the large church steps looking over the centre of the plaza and enjoying the late afternoon sunshine coming in from the west. He is trying not to think of the old Arab Castle at top of the hill, reached by two converging roads, one wide and one narrow leading off opposite corners of the square.

The castle dates back to Moorish times and provides a magnificent view of the surrounding countryside. It is also the site of the Municipal cemetery. Although Luis was born after the Civil War ended, the older generation talking in hushed voices about the atrocities that were perpetrated there, has not escaped his attention. He is also well aware that among the village population, there are certain people who lost relatives during the conflict and certain families whose members may have been part in perpetrating the violent acts.

Opening his bag of purchases from the charity shop he withdraws a pair of Buddy Holly like dark rimmed glasses and a slim discreetly striped jacket. He removes his cloth cap, dons the classes and jacket and feels ready to face the world and pay tribute to his musical hero.

Slowly walking from lower to upper square a few people stop to look, but he feels safe in his disguise and soon settles down at a pavement table at his favourite west facing bar, "El Moro" overlooking the Town Hall building with its clock giving the wrong time as usual.

"What can I get you?" the waiter asks, not recognizing Luis without his cloth cap. Luis orders a Café con leche. This is unusual for Luis as he likes a beer or a glass of red wine.

He sits and watches as the villagers starts to emerge after their midday siesta. Slowly at first, but as the sun goes down it is still pleasantly warm for a February afternoon, the late sun warming the facades on the east side of the square where Luis is sitting, looking he hopes as an reincarnation of Buddy Holly. Soon many of them will be going back to work as the workday is normally broken into two parts; nine to two and five to nine for non-office workers, six days a week while office and public employee workers normally only work eight to two five days a week. Something to strive for, but Luis has never had the urge to live the regulated if easy life of a functionary employed by the regime.

Luis is a good hearted dreamer who can never do enough for his friends. He will spend his last peseta to help if he can. A non-malicious practical joker he is well regarded by his peers.

His Carnaval companions begin to emerge from various side street directions. Not one is fooled by his disguise, knowing this joker too well.

Daniel arrives first and in his usual generous way, offers to buy a round. Luis opts for a quinto. As is his custom, he picks out one of the thin paper serviettes from its holder and cleans the top of the beer bottle which sometimes accumulates a bit of rust or dirt from the metal top. A Quinto is a popular size, a fifth of a litre, the same as a caña. Spaniards prefer this small size of beer, as it can be finished long before it gets warm. And of course one can have so many more without getting drowsy.

Soon all six are present and they shoot the gentle breeze of the late afternoon. Still mourning the death of their heroes but appreciating Luis's tribute, the talk soon moves on to other matters.

Chapter 3: Discussing future plans

Their lives having changed earlier in the day, the group starts reminiscing about the past and venting their still uncertain plans for the future when they will be released from school in a few months' time.

The last days at school are days of uncertainty about the future characterized by a complex mix of repression, resistance, and the anticipation of change.

But that is still four months away. For the moment they have to first concentrate on winning first price in the Carnaval. This is not their first attempt, but this year they feel confident of winning. They have had their spies out to collect information on the other groups and so far, the future looks rosy.

Gabriel suggests spicing up their satirical song with a bit of Buddy Holly rock rhythm like his hit song 'Rave On'.

"I can pick that on my guitar" says Filipe and proceeds to play some cords right there in the square. Horrified, Luis tells him to stop. He likes the concept but does not want the game given away before the event.

Excited, they quickly decide to retreat to Luis's house to rehearse this new idea and to see if it fits in with the traditional Carnaval song framework.

The rehearsal goes very well. The Rave tune allows them to add some good rhythm into their song. They keep improving on it and all agree that this will work on the day. Luis then suggests they all try to find a pair of dark heavy framed glasses they can wear to add some fun to the theme. Never mind the prescription. They can always take the lenses out. It is the image that matters.

"What if I could make a couple of imitation guitars out of some scrap wood from my parent's outhouse?" Angel says. A good idea, they all agree. They can mime while Filipe gives them real guitar support.

They will soon have the beginning of their first group or band. All excited they start talking of touring all of Spain earning loads of pesetas, maybe going to America as well.

It is nice to dream, life is dreary enough with the limited possibilities for enjoyment under the present regime. But first they have to win first price at the Carnaval.

For the next week they keep rehearsing and refining their act. Gabriel and Alejandro get to perform with the guitars made by Angel, standing at either end of the group while Filipe will be in the middle making the real music. He will be flanked by Luis and Daniel blowing their Pito de caña or reed whistles. Angel will be in charge of the twirling the traditional rattle, specific to this part of Andalusia. They will all sing their prepared satirical song and their aim is to be a proper Chirigotas group, walking the streets of the village on Carnaval day and performing wherever they can draw a crowd. And of course win first price. Winners will be announced at the fountain in the main square at the end of the day.

Chapter 4: Ángel the Handyman

Ángel is the one that does not naturally belong in the group as he has not been born in the village but has arrived with his parents from nearby Antequera, a town some 50 kilometers to the north and very difficult to get to due to narrow dangerous winding roads. An old market town, it can lay claim to a large castle, several pre-historic burial sites and the nearby El Torcal. The Lovers Rock dominates the town and is also known as the Montaña Del Indio, due to the resemblance of an Indian facial profile.

Ángel lives in a large farm building close to the railway linking the village to the capital of the province. The farm is old and slowly falling into disrepair, but has many hidden values to young Ángel who likes to construct things. He wants to become an engineer when he finishes college. Fascinated by how things work, he his always planning one project or other.

The job of constructing two make belief guitars for the Carnaval group he belongs to fades into insignificance compared to the stage scenery he has created for the school where he studies. He is working on finalising the stage setup for the end of term play which will be his last before entering the real world and hopefully gain a place at the university to study engineering.

A big person, strong and with a generous head of hair, he has designs on getting to know the young beautiful girl living next door to the farm. She lives in a large house with turrets and a clock tower. Her front garden is part of a public right of way used for religious processions when the local patron saint is carried across the close by railway lines, around this suburb and returned to the tiny chapel where she will rest for another year.

Another thing that attracts Ángel to the girl is that her family is butchers, specializing in best quality beef imports from around the world and for distribution to many local markets and butcher shops. Ángel himself is a sucker for a large Rib Eye steak with all the trimmings. A match made in heaven he thinks. Now he just has to win first prize, and not just at the Carnaval.

A big person, strong and with a generous head of hair, he has designs on getting to know the young beautiful girl living next door to the farm. She lives in a large house with turrets and a clock tower. Her front garden is part of a public right of way used for religious processions when the local patron saint is carried across the close by railway lines, around this suburb and returned to the tiny chapel where she will rest for another year.

Another thing that attracts Ángel to the girl is that her family are butchers, specializing in best quality beef imports from around the world and for distribution to many local markets and butcher shops. Ángel himself is a sucker for a large Rib Eye steak with all the trimmings. A match made in heaven he thinks. Now he just has to win first prize, and not just at the Carnaval.

Chapter 5: The Day of the Carnaval

Rehearsals as complete as can be, the Buddy Holly group of friends get ready for a day of singing their song while trying to evade the Guardia Civil set on enforcing the rule of law and disrupt any public gatherings.

With many groups expected to take to the streets and with only four Guardia Civil officers in the village, a relatively easy day is to be expected. This hilltop village is after all situated in the backwaters and not considered overtly political. All everyone wants is to get on with life, have a good time and the chance to down a few glasses of wine in the sunshine.

The concept of a legal drinking age is not as standardized or strictly enforced as it is in many other European countries. It is common for younger individuals, even children, to consume alcoholic beverages, particularly in social and family settings. There are no strict rules regarding drinking age in Spain during the Franco regime. It is also quite rare to see people drinking in excess and become violent. Drinking is done as a part of a social inclusive framework and not as a means to forget and escape.

The morning is cold but the sun is shining on most of the upper square. Breakfast is being served both inside and out on the limited pavement space. Large plates of Churros and glasses of steaming instant chocolate are carried to tables occupied by old ladies in headscarves chatting away loudly. Their husbands are standing at the bar drinking coffee supplemented with glasses of either anise or brandy. The noise is incredible as everyone tries to be heard over everyone else and the sound reverberates of the high ceiling and the tiled floor littered with used paper serviettes. Cigarette smoke hangs in the air, the lazy ceiling fans having a hard time shifting it. The noisy atmosphere is amplified by the hissing steam from the coffee machine where milk is heated. Banging of the used coffee container being emptied into the large metal bin between brews only add to the total.

Nobody pays when ordering. Either a tally is kept written with chalk on the bar top in front of the gentleman standing there or as far as the tables are concerned, nothing is written down. The waiters keep a tally in their head and very rarely do they get it wrong. Sometimes they may ask a table what they have had and their answer is accepted without any query. Trust among village people is very high and cultivated. Having said that, if anyone is caught cheating, then word gets around to the other bar owners and that person is either banned or made to pay cash on delivery. No mercy.

As the town hall clock strikes midday, Luis and his group know they still have time to get ready before the twelve o'clock start. They are assembled at the mouth of the downward sloping street, catching the sun on their back. The south side of the square is still in the shade due to the tall buildings and the low sun in its orbit at this time of the year. They keep a sharp eye out for other more daring groups and of course for the officers of the Guardia Civil in their green uniforms and funny black patent leather tricorne or three-cornered hat with a raised back plate. This headgear is not something especially associated with the Franco regime, but dates back to the founding of this discipline in the late 1880's.

"Here we go." says Luis and the group enters the upper square feeling a bit silly in their getup but nothing ventured, nothing gained. They are after all after first prize and a hard day's work lies ahead.

They line up in front of the biggest bar and start to sing and perform their act. The older generation look at them, frown, shake heads and carry on chatting. This is not working. Not traditional enough. They decide to go indoors, stand just inside and try again. Same result. First prize is slipping away.

Looking downcast and down hearted, they quickly retreat into the sunshine. "Let's try by the fountain." suggests Luis. Off they trundle, hardly lifting their feet as they walk off, feeling totally defeated.

The younger generation has by now woken up and is slowly making their way towards the village center.

As Luis's group gather their courage and start on their song for the third time, they look on in surprise as the young boys and girls in front of them start to gyrate and dance to this new rhythm. Encouraged by this, the wooden guitars are given an extra beating; Filipe plays for his life, with Luis and Daniel on either side blowing their reed whistles sing their heart out with the rest of the group while Ángel twirls his rattle keeping an eye out for the law.

Chapter 6: Daniel comes out of the closet

Gentle Daniel has known for a long time that he has homosexual tendencies. As in most of the world, this is either frowned on or considered downright illegal. In some countries it is punishable by death, in others by imprisonment and in yet others chemical castrations are performed. Daniel does his best to hide this side of his character. His friends though see right through him and always protect him when necessary.

Though difficult, it is possible to catch a train from the local station to the province capital and from there to travel by local bus to Torremolinos. This seaside town being the acknowledged cultural center for the homosexual community is where Daniel on occasion travels to during school holidays.

Over the last few years, when he has managed to escape the scrutiny of his family and been successful in catching one of the infrequent diesel locomotive trains transporting agricultural or construction material which stops locally, he has spent several days enjoying the relative feeling of freedom with his acquired like-minded friends on the Costa.

Daniel's family live in a large house midway between the upper and lower square where the two roads used for Easter processions meet, connect by steps and then separates again to form a circuitous route allowing processions to move forward without colliding. On one evening and night during Easter, as many as six processions move through the streets of this hill village at any one time.

As is the case with many well to do families, apart from their town house, Daniel's family also owns a finca outside of town. This one is located a few kilometers north and on a sloping hillside below the convent that includes the church where the Patron Saint of this village spends 50 weeks of the year. She is known as Virgin de Flores and she has been the village Patron Saint for near on 500 years.

During the hot summer months, Daniel and his family escapes to this finca where they enjoy the cool hillside breeze and the pleasant view over the river valley below. The finca has been the scene of many successful barbecues over many years.

The family relocating here during the hot summer months makes it easy for Daniel to go into the village on the pretence of meeting friends and staying in the family home but then escape for some days to the costa.

Daniel's younger brother wants to be a doctor and his mind is focused on studying people trying to determine their state of health. Over the past year as they grow into young men, he has noticed a feminine side to his older brother.

Confronting Daniel with this issue, his brother concedes that the future doctor is correct. Asked if they should tell their parents, Daniel smiles and says that they already know and have no problems whatsoever with this, providing Daniel is discreet for everyone's sake and safety.

Matter closed.

Chapter 7: Carnaval winners and losers

As the day progresses, Luis's group collect a growing crowd of young followers as they walk from bar to bar singing their song. Filipe knows a few more American songs made popular by Buddy Holly and though the lyrics are not easy to sing and fit into their limited Carnaval repertoire, the rhythms are easy to reproduce and the group give it their all. They are frowned on by the older population and the rival Carnaval groups prefer to keep their distance.

Come judging time which is way after dark and held in the shadows of the stone lions, all groups gather to hear the verdicts. The Guardia Civil knows when to keep their distance as nearly the whole village is now assembled in the square.

The village mayor has declined to be involved in order to save his skin. He is after all not elected but installed in office by the regime. No political parties are allowed during Franco's regime but a figurehead is still needed to project authority control.

A prominent solicitor and a wealthy citrus grower have agreed to do the judging. They have no fear of regime reprisal as they are both needed to make things function on a day to day basis.

Calling for calm and quiet, they step up on a cast-iron bench and announce the winner of the three hundred pesetas first prize. Second prize is 200 pesetas and runner up will receive 100 pesetas. Not bad for a day's work.

Waiting anxiously, Luis's group miss out on first prize. Second prize is not theirs either. And neither is third prize.

Their act is obviously too unorthodox for this traditional hilltop village, never mind one being ruled by a fascist authoritarian regime.

Luis and his group return to Luis's parent's house, tails between their legs and though defeated retain a degree of pleasure, knowing that the youth of the village were on their side. There is always next year after all.

Chapter 8: A closer look at Alejandro

Where Luis is a sort of laid back placid person, Alejandro by contrast is a young rebel. The two of them have formed a long lasting friendship, maybe because they are so different or because they both share a penchant for mischievousness.

Luis is the practical joker and Alejandro the impromptu action man.

With his corpulent figure, big smiling face and hair in a ponytail Alejandro has many friends in the village. Young and old take to this diminutive giant.

He lives with his parents above one of the few restaurants in the village. As is normal in a hillside village with narrow streets, the entrance to the property leads immediately to a set of steep stairs. No entrance hall or corridor. You step in and you walk up.

Upstairs though there is a great view over the river that snakes its way to the Mediterranean. Below and around the foot of the village, the valley is covered in orange, lemon and olive groves. These groves form the mainstay of the local economy, exporting crops to the world beyond and providing much needed seasonal work for the village population. Steam driven or diesel locomotives pulling long rows of goods waggons stop regularly at the station far below the village. Loading agricultural produce provides yet more local income.

Alejandro's parents do not have a finca in the Campo. Instead, Alejandro spends the hot summer months walking the hills and mountains behind and above the village. His passion is food and he especially likes hot spicy food. That being said, hot and spicy is no good without the addition of herbs like wild thyme, rosemary, oregano, coriander or fennel.

He likes to pick or collect his own olives from trees growing wild on the hillsides. Always carrying a long stick and a large square of netting which he lays out under the olive tree, he beats the branches with his stick and then carefully collects all the fallen olives. His speciality is called Hog Año or this year's first pick. Normally they are picked late September before the olives ripen too much and start to turn blue, purple or black.

Once home, he bashes each one with a small hammer, breaking the skin but leaving the stone. The locals call these olives Maltratados or abused. After a few weeks in frequently changed saltwater brine, the acidity has been removed and it is time to add flavor and put them in sealed containers. Alejandro likes to add thyme and rosemary to some and others he spices up with crushed chili peppers. Most jars also contain a generous amount of peeled halved garlic cloves.

When ready to eat, a jar at a time is offered to his favorite bars in exchange for a generous supply of cañas. This village runs on the barter or cash free principle. It is much easier to avoid a tax bill that way as you have not earned an income.

This being Alejandro's last year at school, he has to decide what he wants to do to survive as he does not want to be too large a burden on his parents. It is OK to carry on living at home as many children do, sometimes into their thirties or forties when one or both parents become ill and need caring for or die and the property passes on to the next generation. If there are many children, this invariable results in lengthy battles over the inheritance. As Alejandro only has one older brother with whom he gets on well and their parents are in good health, no problems loom on the horizon yet.

Chapter 9: School's out. What next?

The disappointment of not winning a prize at the Carnaval soon fades into distant memory.

Spring turns into summer and it is getting hotter by the day. Soon the last school day approaches. And then it is over. This group of friends says a sad farewell to each other with promises of keeping in touch. Then they go their separate ways. Ángel downhill, Luis and the rest uphill before they too split up left, right and straight on.

They have of course talked about what they would do or would like to do, many times over the recent past as the day gets closer.

Alejandro would like to spend a year travelling the world, to see what is happening in the free world. He has Asia and Australia in his sight, but realises that speaking only Spanish and in a hard to understand dialect at that, and with only song lyrics in English at his disposal he will have a hard time managing to survive.

Always an impromptu action man, he is not worried, always willing to take a chance.

Gabriel has his sight set on owning a Bodega. That's it.

Filipe wants to play his guitar and would like to travel to Rumania to learn their language. Nobody can understand why this might be. What use could the Rumanian language be in the future after all?

Ángel as we know as his sight on the beauty next door to his parent's ramshackle farm building. Apart from being a good handyman, he is also good with figures and he thinks good at selling. So he dithers between being an accountant or an insurance salesman. Studying engineering would be nice, but money is scarce. Accountancy takes a lot of time and money to learn, whereas selling insurance can bring instant rewards if he can find a firm to work for in this backwater. The capital may be an option.

Daniel just wants a quiet life with his friends. Torremolinos is his goal.

As for Luis, ever the dreamer and always plotting improbable scenarios, he is happy to sit back outside his favourite bar, El Moro, and see what comes along.

Sitting there in the sunshine one day, he is in awe of some of the older village people, infirm with arthritis or suffering from shortness of breath, braving the steep village streets. They struggle on, but never give up no matter how much pain they may be experiencing. The flat of the square gives them a little respite and leaning on sticks, or pushing old rusty walking frames, wheels or not, one step at a time they make their way from where they came to where they want to go. It may take hours but they persevere.

When a stranger to the village sits himself at the table next to Luis and orders a coffee and a sandwich in broken Spanish, Luis asks him his name, which turns out to something incomprehensible in a foreign language. Luis decides to call him Pepe; easy to pronounce and easy to remember. The coffee arrives but not the sandwich. Pepe looks confused but Luis signals him to be patient. El Morro does not have a kitchen so food is ordered in the bar next door, accounts settled at the end of the day. His food soon arrives, local Serrano ham in a toasted pitufo bun.

Asked what he is doing so far from civilization Pepe says he is looking for a friend he met on the Costa, Sergio his name.

So you are one of them, thinks Luis; Daniel's crowd. Never mind, there is room in this world for all kinds, he muses philosophically but says nothing. As far as he knows Sergio is a painter, not of houses but of things. Putting things on canvas, that cannot be very profitable, but who cares. Live and let live, that is Luis's attitude to life.

Inquiring whether Pepe is an artist, Luis gets a shrug in return. Not much information to glean from this guiri or franchute.

Eventually Luis points to the furthest south western corner of the square. The corner building where Paqui's ferretería is located; she is closed now and the building is in shade. But there is an entrance door down that side street, the side street where Daniel's parent's town house is situated half way down.

Good luck to them he thinks. Keep discreet and be safe. These are not friendly times for the likes of them.

Chapter 10: Gabriel and Filipe

Singing free form Malagueña flamenco songs and playing the guitar is what these two loves to do.

School is out for the last time and a whole new life is in front of them. Question is what to do with it?

Gabriel is in no doubt. He has his eye on a basement space just off the main square where he intends to rent space for his Bodega. He wants to be a bar owner with a difference, offering good cheap tapas and rich local wine and Manzanilla, a strong sherry type wine which he and Alejandro sometimes travel the long way to Sanlúcar de Barrameda by bus or a friend's lorry to purchase. They would normally reckon on being away for at least a week, staying with friends along the way.

Once back home in the village, Alejandro's cousin Lorenzo will store the wine in his parent's house just down yet another side street from the main square. Having a huge basement below the house and the rock which forms three sides of the room provides a dry cool storage space, which is ideal. Also it is not far to go, should the Bodega run low on Manzanilla. Over time they have collected a large quantity, ready for the impending end of school and the soon to happen opening of Gabriel's basement bar bodega.

Once Gabriel has his Bodega up and running, it is intended that Lorenzo will be in charge of Tapas; Filipe will provide the entertainment while Alejandro keep them supplied with olives and other spicy products.

Ángel has promised to find some old wine barrels, repair them and paint them black, then fitting circular tops to serve as tables for people to stand their drinks and tapas on while enjoying the impromptu performances in the Bodega.

Opening day arrives and the group of friends wait with baited breath to see if anyone will arrive down the steps into this now cosy bodega lit with candles and the smell of tapas and Manzanilla blending with the soft picking of Filipe's guitar.

They do not have to wait long. In groups of two or more, they traipse down the stairs, soon chatting loudly with friends and consuming the opening day free tapas and glasses of Manzanilla.

Gabriel then sits down on one of the traditional square straight back chairs, seat covered with woven esparto grass. Filipe sits to his left ready to accompany him on his guitar. Between them is a small round table covered in cloth intricately woven in black and red with delicate tassels along the edges. On top is a small vase with a single flower and a glass of water for the singer.

Luis has yet to arrive as has Daniel, but the crowd gets restless and there seems no reason why they should not start.

They start with a song in the Cante Chico format, a light hearted allegria Gabriel has composed for the occasion.

Then onto a few more serious numbers in the Cante Jondo style, paying tributes to friends and family.

Putting down his glass of water while Filipe carries on picking quietly, Gabriel spots among the newcomers an old friend of his from the Campo; one of a well-known flamenco singing family's sons. Lucas is embraced and offered a glass and motioned to take the seat vacated by the new bar owner.

After a few numbers, another would-be singer wants the seat. As is the norm in this village and probably throughout Andalusia, every self-respecting male considers himself a master singer. It is not unusual to hear a person singing loudly in the street as he walks along or suddenly burst into an emotional tune all by himself while standing at a bar enjoying a glass of wine or beer. Never ignored and nearly always appreciated. Polite acknowledgement always follows.

By now Luis has arrived, sporting his usual cloth cap, baggy green corduroy trousers and chequered flannel shirt. With him is Daniel, just returned from Torremolinos and accompanied by a few like-minded friends.

The party in full swing, free drinks and food long having run out, the crowd is happy paying their way and the air is heavy with cigarette smoke and loud conversation, everyone speaking a little louder to be heard over the others. Such is the good life in a hilltop village during the repressive regime of "El Caudillo de España por la gracia de Dios", also known as Franco. The atrocities committed over twenty years ago by both Nationalist Franco supporters and Republicans, friends and neighbors fighting and killing each others are in the past, but never forgotten and never forgiven.

Chapter 11: La Charla

One of the many bars in this hilltop village is called La Charla. Luis and Alejandro are enjoying an early drink before the midday rush starts. This bar is the place for small talk or where you can pick up pieces of gossip. It is a very popular bar with the locals, small, cramped and normally crowded. At peak times it employs three waiters who compete for space behind the bar but somehow manages to serve everyone in record time while keeping a tally on large sheets of paper behind the bar. Each sheet has multiple columns which bear as a heading the name or nickname of the person having ordered the round. At times it gets very confusing when everyone is inviting everyone else to a beer or glass of wine. No prices are entered on these chits, just a tick. Once four ticks have been entered, the fifth is a diagonal cross line. Bar prices are in multiples of the cost of a caña. Tapas cost the same as a caña. Larger portions warrant two or more ticks. The atmosphere is good natured and the noise is overwhelming as everyone wants his opinion to be heard.

Food is available as tapas; either from large metal trays behind the bar, being dished out on small tapas dishes with a piece of bread or from the small vitrina nestling on the bar counter. The house specialty is Gambas Pilpil, a very spicy dish consisting of large peeled prawns in hot oily paprika sauce. Served in a round earthenware dish, it is ordered from the kitchen upstairs where the lady owner presides over the food preparation.

Orders are placed in a small square dumbwaiter, a bell is rung and the person responsible above pulls it up by rope. Once the order is complete, the bell rings twice and the food is lowered and served. More ticks entered under the appropriate heading. Depending on the size of the Pilpil dish, two or four ticks are entered.

The washing up of dishes works in the same way. Dirties are placed in a washing up bowl which when full is ordered upwards for emptying. Glasses are washed in the sink behind the bar.

On this particular day, the sun is shining and reflecting in the clear plastic bags filled with water hanging over the bar, acting as a very efficient insect repellent throughout the year. The crowd has spilled out onto the pavements, one at a steep angle upwards, the other around the corner still in shadows.

Then the bleating of animals is heard and from one of the side streets emerges a tall man dressed in baggy trousers, jumper and a cap. Carrying a stick and sporting a leather haversack over his shoulder, he leads his flock of brown long eared goats into the square, then passing the crowd outside the shaded side of the corner bar and heads for the hills just visible below the village. His animals follow him with not a look at the crowd, some of which are holding their noses. Once passed, a trail of pellet like droppings litter the trail the goats followed across the village square.

Now is a good time to squeeze indoors again and refresh the glasses. Luis and Alejandro stay outside enjoying the sunshine before it gets too hot.

"Look at this", Luis nudges Alejandro and points at a person slowly weaving its way across the square and passing the fountain, stumbles, slips on the goat droppings and crashes head first into the paving stones.

Shrugging, Alejandro says "It's just David, adding yet another bruise to his already battered forehead."

True enough, David slowly gets to his feet and continues towards the corner bar. Blood drips from his forehead but otherwise unharmed, possibly because as is his way, he is a bit intoxicated at the time of his fall. A frequent visitor to the local doctor, nobody pays too much attention to him or his injuries. He is however always treated well by the village people and quite often one or other will buy him a beer. His village dialect is very difficult to understand, and probably only bartenders and his two brothers understand anything of what he says.

Luis and Alejandro step aside, so David can enter the bar. He has a tab in this bar, and a caña is served. The owner knows that once a month, the tab will be settled. Where the money comes from, nobody queries nor cares about.

Chapter 12: Meeting Daniel's Friends

Daniel, just returned from Torremolinos and accompanied by a few like-minded friends enjoyed the opening of Gabriel's bodega. They are a mixed bunch, Spaniards most of them, from all over the country attracted to the Costa del Sol for its climate; cultural, seasonal or other draws. Some have moved down from the town of Sitges on the Costa Brava, lured not only by the climate but also by the vibrant community embracing like-minded thinking. One blond Irishman is amongst them. Going not surprising, by the name of "Irish" he is a jolly fellow whose only regret is that he cannot get a pint of Guinness when he wants one.

This is their first visit to the village and so far they like it. The natives do not seem to have a problem with their attitude to life and treat them as equals.

The foreign chap that Luis met at El Moro and decided to call Pepe as his name was too difficult to pronounce and to remember, is not one of Daniel's friends yet. Sergio is though and it seems impossible that they will not meet up soon.

Daniel has planned a get together at his parent's finca to coincide with the Romeria pilgrimage dedicated to the patron saint of this village. Always held on the first Sunday following the eight day of September, it is expected to be a somewhat subdued event as although the regime allows religious events, having fun is not something that is publicly encouraged. Which is why, Daniel plans to hold a good singing and dancing party at the finca instead, away from prying eyes of the Guardia Civil.

A large buffet has been laid out indoors away from the hot sun and in the courtyard a small pig is roasting slowly on a spit over a log fire. Next to that is an old bathtub filled with sand three quarter full. Topped up with charcoal now slowly burned to glowing cinders, bamboo skewers will be placed in the sand, at an angle and holding 6-8 fresh sardines each.

Close friends and a few neighbors have arrived early to help with the extensive food preparation. Things are coming together and as early afternoon is approaching nearly everything is ready. Slowly the invited guests start to arrive. Many are in traditional flamenco outfits. The women wearing colorful figure hugging dresses with several layers of flaring skirts down at knee level. Polka dots, floral prints, or solid colors like red, black, or white dominate the designs. Delicately designed shawls draped over arms or shoulders complete the tantalizing vision as does the elaborate hair does decorated with large combes or a clavel. Finally large earrings complete the picture of a true Andalusian woman.

As for the men, in complete contrast to the world of birds where they dominate the roost and flaunt their colors, some are dressed in traditional wide-brimmed hat (sombrero Cordobés) and a vest or jacket paired with fitted trousers and leather boots. The colors are dark green or black, but subdued so as not to upstage their partners.

Normally a party like this would not call for such an elaborate getup but most have come from the nearby feria ground after having delivered the patron saint safely to her chapel where she will spend another year before it is time yet again to repeat the procedure. Daniel's invitation sounds a lot more interesting than standing in a dusty crowd drinking beer and pretending to have fun without any music or dance.

Last to arrive is the Torremolinos crowd led by Sergio and introducing his friend and fellow painter which Luis has christened Pepe due to his unpronounceable French name. Daniel has no problem with the name as over the years on the Costa he has met a variety of people from all over the world.

About fifty people have now gathered at the finca and already a lot of impromptu dancing of the Sevillana is happening.

This is a traditional folk dance which girls learn at a very young age. Its main movements resemble the picking of an apple, turning to offer it to your partner and then throwing it away. This explanation is very simplified as the elegant movements of two accomplished Sevillana dancers defy description. It has to be watched and experienced in person.

Luis and Alejandro are not part of this gathering but are spending time in the village with friends, including Martin, he of the furniture shop.

They miss the excitement, when after a good long lunch one of the guests fails to leave. He looks the worse for wear and is left alone reclining in his chair to hopefully recover and make his own way home later. His name is Jose and he is known to be a Franco Nationalist sympathiser and suspected of having taken part in the atrocities perpetrated at the castle during the Civil War. Although these events are only whispered about behind closed doors now over twenty years later, there are those who consider themselves Republicans and cannot forget the past easily.

Later in the night, when Jose is still in his chair, apparently asleep and not having moved at all, one of the Torremolinos crowd staying over, goes to investigate. After a good poke to the shoulder to try and wake him up, Jose falls to the ground dead. A close by cushion is put under his head in a misguided attempt to make him more comfortable.

Someone is sent up to the village to alert the Guardia. There is no doubt though that Jose is dead as is now confirmed by Daniel's brother, the future doctor.

After establishing that there are no suspicious circumstances surrounding the death, the corpse is carried out and the Guardia leaves.

Chapter 13: La Matanza

Luis wants to organize a Matanza. He has a day in November in mind and puts out feelers among friends and neighbors as to the best weekend for this festive event. Festive that is for the villagers but not for the pig chosen as the lead character.

Both Luis and Alejandro are making preparations for the forthcoming Matanza. It will be held in a large finca below the one that hosted the September festivities. This one is for Campo people and not for faint-hearted town folks.

Sometimes the pig is killed using a metal spike held against its forehead and rammed with a large long handled wooden mallet, the large size important so as not to miss the spike and cause unnecessary suffering.

At other times, as is the case here, the pig is put on a wooden trestle table and calmed by stroking and cooing to ensure an adrenaline rush does not ruin the meat. The throat is then cut while the pig is held firm to enable the collection of blood into buckets for making the famous Morcilla sausage. One person is assigned the important task of stirring the blood to stop it from coagulating before others have cleaned and prepared the intestines and mixed the ingredients of finely chopped belly fat, cooked rice, herbs and spices.

This finca has a walled courtyard with its own well and plenty room for the large wooden scalding tub used for softening up the pig skin after the killing.

As this tub is made of wood and assembled from slats, it will dry out from year to year. In order to make it watertight, it is repeatedly filled with water a few days before for the wooden slats to expand enough to create a perfect vessel for the scalding water.

Large tripods are holding metal pots suspended over log fires. They will be used for the boiling water for the tub. When the pig is lowered into its final bath, it is essential that the temperature of the water is neither too hot nor too cold. It must soften and loosen the hair without damaging the skin. This normally takes a few minutes after which the pig is suspended from a ladder and the skin is scraped for all hair and other impurities. Once cleaned and dried, it is opened up from head to tail and the innards collected.

The most critical part of the Matanza is the making of the Morcilla. The blood has been stirred constantly since it was collected, the casings have been cleaned, the main ingredients prepared. Now comes the slow pouring of pig's blood into the mix while stirring until the consistency is perfect for pouring or stuffing into its final destination. Both ends tied off, the Morcilla is lowered into gently simmering water for about half an hour. Then cooled and stored for consumption during the approaching winter.

Nothing is wasted. Even ears, tail and trotters are considered delicacies among country folks. Hooves are being boiled down for gelatin. The two hams or thighs are put into a below ground salt cellar where they will stay for a few weeks before being hung in the curing or drying loft. A well ventilated cool space this will be their home for upwards of twelve months.

The rest of the pig having been cut into pieces for preserving or minced for sausages for curing or smoking, it is time for the most important part of the Matanza event. Celebrating the successful completion of sacrificing the pig and enjoying some of the products washed down with good wine.

Everyone moves from the courtyard to the garden area below the finca. A good spread has been prepared and there is no shortage of beverages.

The celebrations continue until well after dark when people slowly start their long walk home. Nobody passes by the courtyard and the drowned body in the scalding tub is not discovered until the following morning.

Chapter 14: A closer look at the village people

At any one time, sitting quietly on the sunny side of the square enjoying a morning coffee and a churro, village people will pass the square going either north or south, depending on their type of work. Office and shop workers would generally walk northwards to the business part of the village. Agricultural workers would walk south and downwards to the railway station and the surroundings orchards and groves that provides the mainstay of the village economy.

Among this crowd of industrious people, there are a few that stands out as special individuals.

The diminutive figure of Simón, a happy small person who takes his punishment with quiet stoicism, wanders the streets trying to stay out of harm's way. People seem to have developed a passion for giving him a friendly slap around the top of his head. He takes it in his stride and is often offered a caña in return for the slapping.

Davina is another local curiosity, sometimes referred to as Rubber Face. In her advancing years she has accumulated some additional body weight bending her legs outwards at the knees. Calf length black stockings seem to be her trade mark. Her weather worn face has developed quite a few more wrinkles over the past few years to disguise the fact that in her youth she was a real beauty. She has a heart of gold and always great friends with a big toothless smile and a glint in her eyes.

Pepe is the oldest of the so called ugly brothers. David, Pepe's younger brother who stumbled on the goat droppings earlier in the year is still getting into trouble caused by his love for drinking and his face, arms and legs bear ample evidence of this infliction. Sergio is the youngest of the three. He also is not exactly a pretty face and mostly keeps to himself around the lower square. At night, he is part of the crew that collects refuse from various sites around the village six nights a week.

Pepe in contrast to his siblings is industrious and not work shy at all but also enjoys a drop of alcohol. He is a willing helper when it comes to setting up for refreshments at fiesta times and during Easter. Sometimes short tempered but always generous he is a well-known face in the main square. He has been observed guiding his ancient father for a slow walk in the sun. He cannot be all bad.

Yet another Luis, this one is seriously crippled, probably since childhood, but runs a kiosk selling sweets, toys and magazines just off the main square. Cigarettes are sold from under the counter. Known as Luis el Del Kiosco, a poet, painter and, above all, a very great person he struggles twice a day from his home on the outskirts of the village using his two wooden crutches. He sits in his kiosk, barely able to look over the counter, nor out the serving hatch. His only son does what he can to help his father cope with the hardship life has dealt him.

El Granjero del Manito's, even though he is small and of slight build is considered quite a Romeo by the young females of the village. Maybe because he still has all his teeth and warm lively hands. Hence his nickname. He lives on a farm north of the village and travels in by moped. Often carrying vegetable produce in his panniers which he freely exchange for cañas in the various bars he frequents. The more vegetables, the more cañas. It is often quite a site when he tries to mount his moped late afternoon for his ride home, but early enough to avoid the Guardia Civil who are still observing their siesta.

Golden Pepe is the best dressed person in the village. Often adorned with golden trinkets, be it a chain, necklace or large rings, he wears his suit and tie plus often a red carnation as he walks the village streets. What few people are aware of is that living in the valley below and across the river, he rolls up his trouser legs, take of his leather shoes and cross the shallows barefoot before walking the steep road leading up to the center. Once again looking the immaculate dandy.

Simón, the nearly blind lottery seller is a volunteer with the Spanish ONCE lottery, also known as the Organización Nacional de Ciegos

Españoles (National Organization of Spanish Blind People). This organization was started soon after the Civil War ended to help people in the aftermath who were suffering blindness, disabilities and unemployment. Now over twenty years later it is still going on and the nightly draw and affordable ticket cost gives Simón a decent commission income. Walking along, his white stick searching out obstacles, he wears a vest from which hangs an enormous amount of unsold tickets. He has a week's supply on him, with braille raised dots.

Chapter 15: Local Business

Manolo the Charcoal Vendor has a small shack in the hills above the village. Approached via a steep track, only the occasional visitors come his way. He lives alone with his three dogs who bark loudly when anyone approaches. Alejandro and Luis though can walk past without being accosted by the dogs. They are frequent walkers in these parts, mostly on their own. Alejandro searching for herbs and Luis a keen forager of mushrooms.

Charcoal burning is an art and Manolo is an expert. Throughout the spring, summer and autumn he accumulates sacks of good quality charcoal. When it is time the villagers start feeling the oncoming winter he does a good trade leading his horse and cart through the narrow village streets announcing his product in a loud voice as he walks along. Doors open ahead of him, people gather from side streets and trade is brisk.

Burning charcoal indoors is not without risk. By way of keeping warm during the winter months, people tend to restrict themselves to one room. Sitting at a big round table which has a base supporting a brazier where they burn their charcoal while covering the table and themselves with heavy blankets creating a cozy warm atmosphere. Ventilation is important and it has been known that whole families have died from carbon monoxide poisoning sitting like that due to lack of ventilation.

It is not unusual for one neighbor to knock on another neighbor's door to ask if they have started burning, and if so, have they got any ashes to spare for starting up the next brazier.

Martin is a business and shop owner. He owns the only furniture store in the village. A good friend of Luis and Alejandro; even though he is few years older they still meet up for a quiet drink at times, but business demands that shop comes first. Martin is not much for large gatherings and prefers to stay home or visit his favorite bar at fiesta times.

Not many cars or lorries enter the village. Mostly donkeys or mopeds are used for transporting goods within the village. This may be due to the narrow streets not having been designed for large vehicles. As autumn and winter approaches, one small lorry does make its round the village carrying firewood. Mostly olive but sometimes lemon trees are chopped up as groves are torn up and new trees planted.

Salvador owns this small lorry, a three wheeler with an open cargo bed. He has a small plot of land just outside the village. It is south facing and ideal for drying out green wood. From spring to autumn, he collects wood from orchards that have been replanted. His specialty are the roots which burn longer but unfortunately are more difficult to store in the village outhouses due to the fact they do not stack as easily as straight cut branches. Roots also contain a certain amount of soil lodged between the tendrils. This soil tends to produce a lot of festive sparks during burning. Salvador takes advance orders and with his small lorry, he can easily navigate the narrow village streets. His noisy two-stroke vehicle precedes him and his customers are used to listen out for when their order will be delivered by this polluting means of transport.

Ricardo is a renowned small bird breeder. Canaries breeding is his passion but also a lucrative business. He frowns on villagers who keep goldfinches in far too small cages where they can hardly turn around, let alone hop to another non existing perch. This unfortunately is all too common and frowned on by responsible breeders.

It is not uncommon to see chaps in the square with a bird cage containing up to a dozen canaries they intend to sell. Three story cages have also been spotted to much amusement of by-passers.

In what is locally called Barbers Corner, the two brothers Andrés and Sebastián have been cutting hair for years. Their shop has a wide open front door and chaps very often enter, not for a haircut but for a chat. It is a popular place for the older gentlemen of the village to gather and shoot the breeze.

There are two hardware shops coexisting not too far from each other. In one, Paqui waits patiently for customers while tending to her knitting behind the counter. The other one has two chaps on duty but do not appear to sell more than Paqui does.

People tend to have their preferences so both do good business. It is not uncommon for someone to walk in showing the owner a single screw or bolt asking is they can buy just one more like it. Lots of minor items are sold in very small quantities. But as the saying goes, one céntimo piled on top of another soon amounts to a peseta. From there on the sky is the limit but unfortunately still very high up and very much out of reach.

Survive they do though even with the competition from the new arrival of small Moroccan owned bazaars which manages to cram in an incredible number of items into a small space.

Chapter 16: Rumors and whispers

Following the two recent deaths, barely a month apart, rumours start to circulate through the village. Theories abound but the main consensus being that this is the beginning of a vendetta. What started during the Civil War when neighbors were killing neighbors for supporting either the Nationalists or the Republicans had in the past twenty odd years been quietly forgotten but never forgiven. Anger still smolders but has so far been contained.

Luis and Alejandro have friends and know families at both ends of this spectrum. They have heard stories of executions in the castle grounds. Also of the terrible death march to Almeria when fugitives were strafed by machine-guns from low flying air crafts. The horror of Guernica has also been told countless times.

Having been born after the Civil War ended but in the latter part of the Second World War in which Spain had maintained neutrality, they are used to hardship and shortages but now, closing in on the decade of the sixties things look a lot easier. So the last thing anyone wants is the resurgence of hostilities in this quiet backwater of a hilltop village.

"Have you any idea if the two deaths were murder or just accidents?" asks Luis. "We were there at the Matanza and saw nothing. The chap that drowned was a known Republican, I know. What about the one that died in his sleep at Daniel's finca?"

"A known Nationalist" answers Alejandro. "I heard they found his head resting on a pillow! Do you fancy investigating to find out what really happened? Who smothered the Nationalist and who tipped the Republican into the tub and held him down?"

"I would leave that to the law, incompetent as they may be," says Luis, "Times are difficult enough without attracting the attention of the Guardia."

The two friends decide to wait and see if more incidents or accidents will happen over the next few weeks or months.

Meanwhile a new decade is approaching and with that hope and expectations of a brighter more enlightened future. It is now nearly half a year since they left school and now considered responsible adults; they will have to find their own way in the world.

Luis for sure will stay around the village and indulge in his passion for a game of chess in between frequent trips into the surrounding hills and mountains to forage for mushrooms. He has also got a keen interest in the Caminito del Rey which is crumbling into disrepair. If only it could be repaired sufficiently to avoid tragedies when daredevils try to walk their way through the gorges.

With the New Year approaching there is a lot of speculation as to when Midnight will occur. This may sound strange but the Town Hall Clock is notoriously inaccurate.

A lot of people will gather in the square clutching their twelve grapes. Following tradition one grape will be consumed for every strike of the infamously inaccurate clock. Rumours have it though that the Mayor himself is behind the controls and that tonight, the last night of the decade he will be the controller of the correct time. Sure enough, for once the clock is adjusted to show the correct time and as the twelve chimes sound, the village people consume their twelve grapes in rapid succession. Big cheers to welcome the Sixties. Who knows what time it will be tomorrow?

No further unexplained deaths have occurred over the past two months, so maybe it was just rumors and whispers after all. One death has occurred recently though but not necessarily suspicious, A chap fell through the bottom of his small balcony down in the gipsy quarter. Apparently the girders holding the balcony had rusted trough and the tiles gave way, resulting in him crashing to the pavement ending up with his head bashed in.

Luis is content in his village square taking sun and drinking a quinto at El Moro bar. He misses Alejandro who at the first opportunity jumped on a freight train and headed for the port of Algeciras. Not easy as the trains' northward route take him through the El Chorro gorge to deposit him in a village and railway junction called Bobadilla. Ten years before, a mail train derailed here killing 8 and injuring many more. Here his aim is to catch a southbound connection and then catch or get himself hired onto a freighter destined for the Far East.

Luis is eagerly awaiting a promised postcard from foreign shores.

Chapter 17: Life carries on

The Sixties are here. Down in Gabriel's Bodega they still indulge in Flamenco music and some of the regulars are venting the idea of forming a Peña society. A Peña is like a social club where members pay to belong. This might seem counterproductive to Gabriel's Bodega until you consider that membership would entitle you to cheaper drinks and on Gabriel's part he would now be subjected to less stringent tax laws. All round a Win-Win situation.

Daniel is still travelling to Torremolinos frequently. He does not seem to lack money. Maybe his friends are supporting him or his parents are generous and that is their way of keeping things quiet.

Filipe continues toying with the idea of going to Rumania to learn the language. But the Bodega keeps him busy and content for the moment.

Angel has started selling insurance, having talked his way into a large company operating out of the capital but also encompassing the rural villages of the province. This means he can carry on living at home and keep an eye on the beauty next door. Once he is firmly established with his own clientele providing royalty income and he has money in the bank, he will make his move.

Television has been available in Spain now for about four years. Restricted to a few hours a day and of course to government control, it is as yet not widespread in the village. Cost is one consideration but the lack of programs that might inspire are competing with the village life routines of dragging chairs into the streets and sit for hours, well into the night, chatting with neighbors and occasionally bursting into some happy songs accompanied with clapping. Clapping or palmas is a very important part of the art of flamenco and is learned from an early age.

As for Luis, he has had no option but to apply for a job with the local council. However much it will curtail his freedom to roam, he has no choice. He has been accepted as a junior apprentice in the accounts department. The hours of eight to two five days of the week suits him. The meagre salary will just keep him in quintos and tapas and he is envisioning a day when he will be able to influence decisions affecting the future of his village.

So all seems to be under control. The four lions are still spouting water, the town hall clock is still showing the wrong time and the seasons keep changing.

Something is in the air though. A sense that the austere government control is easing slightly. The economy is growing due to Franco supporting growth and investment. Outside influence from around Europe has encouraged improvements in the infrastructure and investment in hotel constructions. Tourism is about to take off due to the large sandy beaches, the many hours of sunshine and the rich cultural heritage combined with picturesque landscapes being very attractive to foreign visitors.

As for Alejandro, the occasional postcard arrives at Luis's house telling little apart from names of places visited. He has been gone now for over a year. Luis hopes he will see sense soon and point his nose homewards. He and his products are sorely missed.

Chapter 18: Swings and no Roundabouts

Luis, now settled in his administration job has many hours to spare and has the idea of recreating a swing day as was celebrated in this village before the atrocities of the Civil War ruined all for all.

In the side street where Luis lives, there is a spot where it narrows just before the downward slope begins which leads to the railway station far below.

Here, the villagers in pre Franco times used to stage a summer afternoon and evening event where ropes were tied to the buildings on either side of this narrow gap. A long wooden board was securely tied to the middle part, forming a swing that could hold up to three youngsters. The ropes were decorated with local flowers like hibiscus, oleander and bougainvillea. This event is what Luis hopes to recreate. Luis is getting more and more interested in local folklore, realising slowly that his village has an enormous font of talent, be it music, song, dance, painting, poesy or storytelling.

Having gotten Guardia Civil approval to stage the event, due to Luis quoting his Town Hall status, thereby overriding any official objections, planning gets on the way.

Basic elements are easily obtained by friends who want to help and partake. The relief from dreary day to day life is a powerful incentive.

The sun will be shining of course so tarpaulins has to be erected, tables for food and the inevitable paella cooking pan on a butane powered tripod stand have to be found. Loads of ice has to be made, to keep the drinks cool. A mountain of pincho skewers with pork or chicken marinated in special ingredients will be needed. Pork hamburgers for the butane fired plancha and buns to be filled with tasty local beef egg tomatoes have to be financed. A stand erected to sell tickets to be presented at the food and drinks section keeps the accounting process under control.

Finally music is needed. A local acoustic band, complete with box drums or cajones has promised to entertain free of charge. A verdiales dancing group will also be there for a short while to entertain with lively repetitive guitar strumming, flag throwing girls in traditional costumes and castañetees giving a real Andalusian flamenco feel to the event.

What can possibly go wrong when such meticulous planning has been applied?

Well, luckily nothing did go wrong. The fiesta of the Swing was a great success and apart from actually making a profit on the ticket sales thanks to many generous donations by the village people, Luis is hailed as a good chap, receiving many a clap on the shoulder from his vecinos.

There are talks of making this an annual event of course, happiness running riot as is normal after a successful event. As it turns out though the following year will be the wettest year in living memory.

Chapter 19: Easter Rain

Drought has been stalking the village for a few years and everybody is praying for rain. But please not over Easter. Seems prayers don't always work however hard you try.

For months now the various brotherhoods have been gathering at their headquarters, not spread around the village but concentrated on the two procession routes leading from the parish church in the lower square to the upper square. They had been designing posters, maintaining and mending the expensive robes of Jesus and Mary in their incarnation particular to each brotherhood plus deciding on rank and file importance when leading their particular throne through the village. Also, the male Portadores or Costaleros have to be chosen, tunics measured, repaired or new once sewn. There are no female Portadoras or Costaleras; this is an exclusive male privilege and preserve. With a new intake every year, practice is needed and time is allocated to each brotherhood to practice the art of walking in step while carrying the heavy throne. This normally happens inside the parish church away from prying eyes.

Every so often, a break is needed in this hard work and the officials of whichever brotherhood decides to award themselves with an elaborate dinner.

Finally it is time to reveal their poster for the year and all village dignitaries and other important persons gather in the Parish church to listen to endless speeches by a never ending row of persons happy to hear their own voices. Finally the poster is revealed and then the thank you speeches follow.

After all that hard work, it is not surprising everyone is praying for a dry and sunny Easter week. Even in the middle of a serious drought.

The order in which the Easter passion is played out is not always in strict biblical order, with so many versions of Jesus and Mary moving between churches and chapels. As one villager points out to one of the few tourists that has ventured into this village: "It does not matter if we get the order wrong, the only thing that matters is that we get it all done."

Weather forecasting is rudimentary at best and decisions as to take the thrones out or not is largely based on local knowledge, studying and interpreting clouds, consulting almanacs and contacting friends and relatives downwind to learn what might be coming this way. This year is especially vulnerable to making the wrong decision with heavy cloud cover broken only by occasional glimpses of blue sky.

Palm Sunday a chance is taken and the sun smiles on the village. Later in the week it is a different story with several events having to be cancelled due to heavy downpours. The villagers cry while the farmers smile. Impossible to please everyone.

Chapter 20: Tourism

This village has now got a bus service nicknamed el mataguarros or The Donkey Killer. It is so named because in these narrow village streets there is hardly ever room for both auto-bus and donkey. Donkeys and mules being a much used animal for transporting goods and farmers around, they are not easy to move if they do not want to.

Buses are also used to getting their own way, and where a donkey brays, the bus or more correctly the driver uses his horn to move on and get past an obstacle. These encounters have caused fatalities when the donkey gets scared by the sound of the horn and starts' behaving in a way it was not meant to. Progress is slow to take hold in this village.

There have been times when Luis is sitting in the sun outside El Moro that he has spotted a tourist. A rare site even now that the Costa beaches are attracting busloads of pale northerners. They stand out among the natives in as much as they turn pink and even red when exposed to the southern sun. Much like a lobster being given a bath in boiling water.

The other comical thing to observe is when a family of four one day strays into the upper square. Father in shorts, sandals and white ankle socks leading his wife and two children in tow. Mother and children sporting floppy sun hats, father a straw sombrero. All are pink and stand out as not being from here.

Soon it will be necessary for the bar owners to post English language messages in the toilets asking customers not to throw their used paper down the toilet but put it in the bins provided. That said, quite a few bars still have the hole in the ground type conveniences where you have to squat to do your business. You will have to bring your own paper into these places. Do with it what you will afterwards.

Many villagers refer to the tourists and the odd newcomer as Franchutes irrespective as to what country they are from. Luis as we have seen calls them Pepe, but there are sometimes too many of them, and having a hundred foreigners named Pepe is not practical. So Franchutes has to be good enough.

The odd film crew also gets lost and end up in this village by design or mistake. One film, Holiday in Spain or The Scent of Mystery, has a few scenes from the steep streets in the village. It was the first film known to include Smell-o-vision. Although never seen in Spain and later lost forever, exiting times may lay ahead for this hilltop village. Maybe even fame and fortune. For the time being, there are smells abundant in the air, from Azahar or orange blossoms to the droppings from goats passing through or from the unwashed bodies of some of the chaps shooting the breeze on doorsteps or windowsills. Benches for the citizens to sit and relax on are not yet a priority for the local authorities.

The Franchutes have seen a business opportunity in the village, well actually below the village near the orange groves. They are collecting orange blossoms to distil perfume essence. What that does to the production of oranges, nipping the flowers before there is time to set bud and fruit, is not considered. Once there is enough fragrance to fill a few small bottles, they are off to France to be diluted many folds to be sold at an enormous profit.

Chapter 21: Alejandro is back

Carrying a pile of records purchased during his world adventure, Alejandro steps of the Donkey killer bus in the main square and heads for the El Moro Bar where he spots Luis enjoying the afternoon sun.

"So you are back. And about time too," says Luis jokingly.

Luis feels a bit miserable, too many tourists eroding the quiet life and hard earned traditions in his village. He needs cheering up, and Alejandro is just the person to do it. Or so he thinks.

Alejandro has other ideas. Having himself been a tourist for close on two years, his view of the world has expanded somewhat compared to Luis's.

"Just the other day I saw a group of foreign tourists being dropped of at that end of the village." Pointing to the south west, Luis continues. "They walked straight past the square and continued to the other end of our village. No doubt their bus had skirted our hill and gone to pick them up there. I am sure they did not spend a peseta but still left their litter for us to pick up." Indignant he looked at Alejandro for support, but only got a big smile in return.

"Let us go down to Gabriel's bodega and see if he has a record player." Alejandro is exuberant and wants some action. Rock and Roll is in his blood now, having been outside his village for so long. His pile of records rests on the table between the two friends, and Alejandro is eager to show off his treasures.

Luis on the other hand is not at all fired up by Alejandro's enthusiasm and cannot see what all the fuss is about, let alone what good it will do. He fears more deterioration of village values. We have loads of local talents, who can sing, dance, play guitars, compose poetry and paint pictures. What use have we for these long haired foreigners playing loud metallic music, he wonders.

Anyway, Luis is interested to hear about Alejandro's travels and off they walk to Gabriel's bodega just down a street off the main square.

It is quiet down the Bodega this time of day so they lean on the bar. Luis gets his quinto, wipes the top and throws the napkin in the foot well below the bar. Alejandro has a glass of red wine, not the local stuff which is too sweet for him, but some nice dry from the banks of the river Duero up north. Gabriel has a glass of Manzanilla, his favourite tipple.

They spend an hour listening to Alejandro regaling them with his tales of travel. Then it is time for Alejandro to catch up on local gossip.

There had only been one more suspicious death since he left the village. This one, a murder down in the barriada, a man found beaten to death in the dry river bed. It did not sound like part of the ongoing feuds between the two sides that had faced each other during the Civil War. This was more a crime of passion judging by the state of the corpse. The culprit had still to be apprehended nearly a year later.

"Do not forget the woman committing suicide up at the El Chorro Gorge", points out Gabriel.

"A lovers tiff or unacquainted love," says Luis "Not at all suspicious. The Caminito del Rey is a good spot to jump."

Other than that, things had just trundled along quietly, seasons changing and the sun shining most of the time. Oh, one bit of news: Ángel had finally gotten married to the gorgeous girl next to where he lived in the ramshackle farm building down by the railway line. He had now moved into her parent's house with the turrets and clock tower where he is no doubt eating large steaks every day.

Filipe had managed to get to Rumania for a few months and on his return to the village liked to show off his newly learned language skills. Not too difficult for the locals to grasp as the only words he knows are Da Da and Ya Ya. These were repeated at every possible occasion and he seemed very pleased with his new found skill.

As for Daniel, he seemed to be spending a lot of time in Torremolinos but occasionally returned to the village with five or six of his closest friends in tow.

"That's it as far as updates goes," says Gabriel. Things are easing in the village though; the regime appears more tolerant and outward looking in terms of welcoming investment and attracting tourism. Here a scowl from Luis who is dead set against tourism.

That leaves Gabriel to bring them up to date on his own life.

Chapter 22: Gabriel has itchy feet

The novelty of having his own Bodega is beginning to bore Gabriel. He wants to discover the world, having listened to the tales Alejandro has been telling.

But first he has to transfer the lease of his Bodega. The idea of a Peña did not materialize, so who might be interested?

He breaches the subject with Alejandro. Skeptical and not yet ready to settle down after his travels, Alejandro is afraid of losing his freedom, getting tied to a bar that needs attention at least six days of the week and many hours of the day plus evenings or nights. Then there is staff to consider, especially for the kitchen; a reputable and reliable cook is in high demand as everyone knows what the food should look and taste like. Portion sizes should be just a fraction more generous as what is offered in the other bars in the village without reducing profitability. Bar staff is never a problem, the learning curve not steep at all plus the fact that most customers are village people and known by sight if not always by name.

Gabriel agrees to give Alejandro a few months to think about it. Meanwhile research has been done into an outfit called Club Med which offers good prospects and have centres around the Mediterranean coast has caught his imagination.

Crunch time! Gabriel has been offered a position at the Majorca centre. He wants to go. He wants to go now! Alejandro is pressured and finally gives in, having accepted the free transfer and all stock included, providing the existing staff is retained.

The few formal papers needed are signed at the notary office and Alejandro is now the proprietor of his first bar. He also has a name for it: Las Rejas or The Bars - a play on words as Alejandro knows quite a few English words following his travels. Reason for the name being he has discovered a back entrance from the street at the back, one of the two procession routes used at Easter. This back entrance leads to a small bar called the K for some unknown reason. What is important is the fact that both Alejandro and the proprietor of the Barra K are ardent Rock and Roll enthusiasts so they have reached an agreement to host joint ventures once all formalities are in place.

Gabriel is given a good send-off and life in the village continues as if no world shattering event has just happened.

Chapter 23: Beatlemania and The Rollins

The year is now 1963 and the long haired Liverpool pop group naming themselves 'The Beatles' has captured the world music scene with their catchy songs causing girls to faint wherever they perform. Beatlemania is a concept difficult to define but it has turned the music world upside down.

Alejandro likes it but he is far more intrigued by 'The Rollins'. Their group's red logo of the lead singer's rubber lips are posted around the walls of his newly acquired bar, located below ground off the main Easter procession route.

The Beatles album covers also adorn his walls as do photos of famous contemporary Spanish singers and groups.

The music of 'The Rollins' as he calls them is so much more in tune with his love for Blues, Rhythm and Blues, Soul and of course Rock and Roll. The wilder the better. The louder the better. Good thing his bar is two floors down from street level.

Alejandro has been lucky having acquired the services of a good female cook. Like Alejandro, she loves to cook with lots of herbs and spices. Her pig's cheek dish is famous as is her soup of chick peas and tripe served with generous slices of black pudding. Alejandro has a jar of finely ground hot spicy chili peppers for those clients who like it hot.

On June 13th Alejandro is celebrating his name day, the day of San Alejandro, his patron saint of lost items. Everyone is welcome and Encarnación the famous cook in his employ has agreed to prepare a dish of pig's trotters, tripe and very fatty pork belly. This will be a real treat for the courageous villagers who can stomach such an elaborate feast. Interestingly, not many female villagers seem prepared to partake. It is a mostly male affair but with lot of singing, drinking, back slapping and other boisterous behavior designed to relieve the tension and pressure that a hard village life impose on them.

Alejandro resist the temptation to play his latest Rollins record and is content to let the crowd create their own entertainment using a guitar, anise bottles, Zambomba and whatever impromptu rhythmical items are available.

Never short of ideas for yet another event that will generate money, Alejandro has a reputation for throwing a good party. Whenever he puts up posters around the village to promote an event, they are read with interest and soon people will be coming down his stairs, ready for a good time.

Presiding behind his bar, his now ample belly sometimes gets in the way, but with his wide grin and his greying ponytail he still looks like a friendly diminutive giant.

Chapter 25: Fast forward to 1975

Franco is dead. Long live the King. Village life continues but nothing is the same as when we first encountered our group of friends on "The Day the Music Died".

El Caudillo has been replaced by a King; a King who reportedly shot his own brother by accident; a brother who had been designated by Franco to be the future king of Spain. Let's hope the new King does not shoot anything else.

A quick recap on the group of friends we met fifteen years ago.

Ángel is still happily married and now the proud father of two strapping sons. He is still very fond of a large juicy steak. A new group of friends fill the life of his wife and himself. They are both very active promoting the culture of this village and together with a group of school teachers has formed an association they call 'A well fenced community'. This refers to an ancient poem depicting a time when the Moors tried to attack this village and failed.

Sadly both Daniel and Filipe died a while back. They will be and still are sorely missed by their friends.

Gabriel stayed with Club Med for some years but when he met his future wife, a lovely small person with a large amount of energy, they decided to return to his village and start yet another Bodega. Now on his third or is it fourth venture, things seem to be going well for this highly regarded couple. They still frequent Alejandro's bar and recently met up with Luis as well.

Luis unfortunately soon after suffered a heart attack while eating a banana. No connection or suspicious death was recorded. In his short lifetime Luis achieved an enormous amount recording and preserving the culture of his beloved village. He raised funds for monuments and statues and was very active collecting signatures for the restoration and preservation of the Caminito del Rey, the walkway through the El Chorro gorge.

One last thing to report: Alejandro has been collecting funds for a chessboard to be erected somewhere in the village as a monument to Luis, a great chess enthusiast who has now played his last game and sadly lost.

About the Author

Born in Denmark, lived 30 years in England. Married to Hazel for nearly fifty years. Both now retired and living in Andalusia since 2004
Read more at https://www.avellanoweb.net/.